the beekeeper

Maxence Fermine

This edition published in the UK by
acorn book company
PO Box 191
Tadworth
Surrey KT20 5YQ

email: info@acornbook.co.uk

www.acornbook.co.uk

ISBN 0-9534205-9-0

British Library Cataloguing in Publication Data.
A catalogue record for this book is available from the British Library.

Translated from the French by Chris Mulhern
First published in France by Éditions Albin Michel S.A.
Copyright ©Éditions Albin Michel S.A., Paris, 2000
This translation copyright © acorn book company, 2004
Printed and bound in Great Britain by The Cromwell Press, Ltd.

We would like to thank the Arts Council
of England for their assistance
in the publication of this title.

This book is supported by the French Ministry for
Foreign Affairs, as part of the Burgess programme
headed for the French Embassy in London by the
Institut Français du Royaume-Uni.

To my grandfather Didier Fermine,
beekeeper

There is no greater thing in life
than that secret sense of harmony
that unites us briefly
with the great mystery of others
and allows us to travel alongside them
for part of the way

Alvaro Mutis

I

1

Aurélien Rochefer was born in a painting of sun and light. A painting called Provence.

When he was a boy, a bee had settled on the palm of his hand. It settled for only an instant before flying away again. But there, across his life-line, it had left a trace of golden-yellow pollen.

From that moment, Aurélien had dreamed about honey and decided that one day he would become a beekeeper.

In 1885, Aurélien was twenty years old, and was thinking about bees. His plan was to build a few beehives and to make honey. He would then become the only beekeeper in Langlade and the honey he sold would be the best in Provence.

In Langlade, lavender meant wealth, and Léopold Rochefer, Aurélien's grandfather, knew that well for he was the largest lavender-producer in the region.

The two men lived alone in an old farmhouse with blue shutters, and all around them were the fields of lavender where the drowse of insects never ceased.

Léopold had found gold in the blue of the lavender. For Aurélien it was in the yellow of honey.

'Each of us has his own colour,' as Clovis used to say. Clovis was the proprietor of The Green Cabaret, the village café. He had found his colour while quenching the pain of his first heartbreak, in a glass of ice-green absinthe.

Honey was precious and colourful, but compared to Clovis' absinthe and Léopold's lavender, it wasn't so valuable. Indeed as the old man kept reminding his grandson:

'You'll never get very far as a beekeeper, Aurélien.

You certainly won't make a living out of it.'

'Let's wait and see,' answered Aurélien.

Eventually, tiring of this discussion he had gone into an old bookshop in Arles, and emerged with a treatise on beekeeping under his arm.

That Winter, he spent his time doing a few repairs around the farmhouse, and weaving beehives out of reeds. In the evenings he sat by the fire and read: *Scenes from the Mysterious Life of Bees*.

Whenever Aurélien spoke about bees, a mysterious glint would appear in his eyes. This rather unsettled his grandfather. But being a man of few words, Léopold kept his suspicions to himself.

That is until one night, having drunk too many absinthes, he found himself confiding in Clovis. Leaning on the counter of the bar in The Green Cabaret, the old man was savouring with pleasure that blessed moment when the essence of ideas is slowly diluted into the alcohol of dreams.

'Ever since he first started talking about becoming a beekeeper, Aurélien has had this strange look in his eyes.'

'What kind of strange look?' asked Clovis.

'Well I don't know, exactly. It's hard to explain. He talks about bees, and he looks at you, but he stares straight through you, as if he's looking at something way off in the distance.'

'If I were you,' answered Clovis, 'I'd let him go on dreaming about bees, for that sounds to me like the beginnings of a dream.'

At the beginning of 1886, Aurélien Rochefer became a beekeeper. Since this was only his first season, he thought that ten hives would be about the right number to begin with.

'Honey is a sun that must be allowed to ripen,' he told whoever was prepared to listen, 'and to make a good sun you need time.'

In the Spring, he came across a swarm in the forest. The bees were massing darkly around the queen, and allowed themselves to be captured easily. Aurélien put them carefully inside a hive and fed them on sugar-water. He had found his first treasure. A few days later, he bought seven more swarms from a beekeeper in Manosque.

'These are the finest bees in the whole of Provence!' the man assured him. 'They came from the Valensole plateau!'

As the days got warmer, myriads of bees took off from the hives and began gathering nectar from the flowers in the fields. Aurélien was entranced by the sight of them flying from flower to flower, from dawn until dusk, in a graceful spiralling dance. He watched them for hours, marvelling at the secret alchemy that could transform the nectar of flowers into the gold of honey.

That Summer, he began his harvest. First he puffed smoke into the hives, then one by one he lifted out the frames, and collected the honey that dripped from the cells. He watched it trickling slowly into a big earthenware jar like molten gold. He had gathered his first crop of honey.

One evening in September he sold his honey to a shopkeeper in Arles, except for three pots that he put aside for himself. And three more that he gave to Pauline.

Pauline was Clovis' niece. She was also the prettiest lavender-seller in the region. In fact she was more than pretty, she was beautiful, and when a man looked into her eyes, an enchantment came over him.

One morning, Pauline was coming back from the market where she had been to sell her lavender essence. She came across Aurélien by the village fountain.

'Well Mr Beekeeper,' she asked him, 'what are you going to do now that the harvest is over?'

Aurélien held her gaze for a long time before answering:

'I'll wait for the Winter I suppose, and build a few more hives.'

For Aurélien, Winter was the hardest of seasons. There was nothing to be done, except wait. To wait for the coming of Spring.

There was no sign of life. The bees were resting inside their hives. But with the tiniest ray of sunlight, a few would come out and warm themselves in the sunshine. While they were buzzing around in the air, they were safe, but as soon as they touched the snow, they perished.

Everything was desperately white. All fruits and flowers had disappeared. The leaves had fallen with the first frosts, and the mushrooms slept beneath a covering of snow. The sun was no more than a pale white disc. And Aurélien's heart was cold, so cold it felt almost lifeless.

Once the new hives were built, Aurélien was overcome with boredom. He went for long walks in the snow-covered woods. By the time he returned the sun had dipped behind the mountains. He would light a fire and begin reading his treatise about beekeeping.

One evening as he sat by the warmth of the fire, Aurélien found himself thinking of the bees in their hives. He thought of them huddling together to keep themselves warm. It seemed to him that the bees had succeeded where men had failed. For the bees in the hive were all working together, they were living in harmony. Whereas little by little, throughout their slow evolution, mankind had been drifting further apart.

And he began to dream of turning into a bee…

Bees can die for the love of a flower.

Bees can die of love.

Bees can...

In fact, we know very little of what bees can do.

One January morning, Aurélien found a dead bee in the snow. It lay there before him, a tiny thing of gold and black. A jewel of fire, in an ocean of whiteness. He picked it up very carefully and placed it in the palm of his hand. But as soon as it touched his skin, it shattered like glass.

He opened his hand, and held it up to the sun, watching sadly, as the golden dust hung shimmering momentarily in the air, and then disappeared in the snow.

Spring was late that year and the hives, like the flowers, lay buried beneath a mantle of snow.

At the beginning of May, the weather changed, and with the first warm days, the bees began their dance of love. The queen of his first hive took off, taking with her a part of the colony, which by this stage had become too large to live under the same roof. The swarm flew for a short while, and then settled on the branch of a nearby cherry tree, where Aurélien was able to re-capture it.

Inside the hive, which now had no queen, the bees began to produce royal cells. Sixteen days later, a new queen emerged and the hive came alive once more. Her first task was to eliminate all the other royal nymphs. This she did without pity. Finally, surrounded by her courtiers, she retired deep inside the hive, where she would spend the rest of her life laying eggs.

The beekeeper now had twenty working beehives, and had doubled his yield of honey. But he still felt a special affection for his very first hive, which that year had given him almost forty kilos of honey.

Clovis, who had stopped by to congratulate him on his second harvest, had the whole fascinating subject explained to him by the new master beekeeper.

'Did you know a queen can lay almost a thousand eggs in a single day. And a new queen, like that one there, for instance, she can lay almost two thousand. And she reigns over forty thousand drones.'

Clovis wasn't sure about these rather technical matters. But he could see all the pots of honey.

'It's as if it's raining gold!' he said.

'It is! It's the gold I've been looking for!'

'And what does Léopold have to say about it?'

Aurélien didn't answer at first. He lowered his head, gazing idly at a bee that was buzzing around him.

'He still says it won't work. He says I'll never manage to make a living out of beekeeping. He thinks it's madness.'

'He could be right.'

'He could be, but this is what I came here to do. To look for gold. Even if at the moment it's only honey.'

'Perhaps you are right, after all.'

'Maybe, who knows? But it seems worth a try.'

'Yes, Aurélien,' agreed Clovis, scratching his head. 'It seems worth a try.'

So the beekeeper's dream was beginning to bear fruit. It seemed that the fates were with him. But then one day, everything changed. Aurélien was replacing the lid on top of a beehive, when he knocked the one next to it with his elbow. The hive toppled to the ground and one of the wooden frames slid out. It was dark with bees. The bees rose up in a fury and attacked him from every side. Within seconds they were swarming all over him.

Aurélien felt the first sting in his arm, a sharp piercing pain. He began to run. But he could not outrun the bees. Again and again they caught up with him. By the time he reached the river, there were stings burning all over his body. He threw himself in. And the water saved him.

Léopold saw him stumbling back, his face all swollen.

'What happened?' he cried.

All Aurélien managed to say was:

'The bees…'

And then fainted in his grandfather's arms.

Léopold carried him up to his room, and laid him

down on the bed. He closed the shutters to keep out the sun, and cooled his forehead with a wet cloth. He took out dozens of stings. Then he brewed a potion of wild herbs and applied it to the wounds. Finally, he gave him a few spoonfuls of propolis, and left him to rest.

That night, Pauline came to watch over him. His poor face was so disfigured that she could hardly recognise him. She took his hand in hers, and held it, all night long.

'Don't die,' she whispered. 'Please don't die…'

Aurélien wanted to open his eyes and look at her, but his eyelids were so swollen he could barely glimpse the light from the candle on his bedside table. He moaned three words that Pauline could not understand, and then he fell asleep.

His delirium lasted two nights, a torment of fever and pain.

When he woke up, on the morning of the third day, the sun was shining high in the sky. The fever had left him. Léopold and Pauline knew that now the worst was over.

'What happened?' asked the beekeeper, in a whisper.

'It was the bees,' Léopold told him.

Pauline smiled, happy to see him regaining his strength. Now at last, he could finally look at her, too. They told him what had happened, and how close he had come to death.

'Don't blame the bees,' he said. 'It was my fault, not theirs.'

He got up, drank a glass of milk, ate some bread and honey, took a last spoonful of propolis, and went off to visit the beehives.

From then on, Aurélien was immune to the poison of a sting. And neither bee nor wasp, nor even hornet could harm him. In fact, it seemed as if he had overcome suffering altogether.

'What exactly is propolis?' Pauline asked him sometime later.

'That was what saved my life,' answered the beekeeper. 'Come with me, there's something I want to show you.'

He took the girl by the hand and led her towards the hives. When they got there, he showed her the tiny bubbles of resin that sealed the hive and kept out the cold.

'This is propolis,' he said. 'It heals wounds, and can be used for all kinds of aches and pains. They say that Stradivarius even used it to seal his violins, which was why they had such a perfect tone.'

Pauline was amazed that the same thing could be used for violins or injuries.

'So, it heals the wounds of the body as well as those of the soul?'

'Yes,' said Aurélien, 'and in either case, it works miracles!'

So the bees produced propolis and honey. But that wasn't all. More wonderful still was the food on which the queen herself was fed. Royal jelly.

'If all I ate was royal jelly,' Aurélien used to say, 'then I think I could live forever.'

Pauline thought this was nonsense.

'And if I ate royal jelly, what would happen to me?'

'After sixteen days, you would become a queen!'

Aurélien Rochefer went on tending his bees and, by the third year, he had a hundred thriving beehives.

1888 was a terrible year. There was frost in April, hail in May, and then drought in August. Each took its toll. The harvest was ruined. The price of maize doubled, that of wheat tripled, and that of lavender-honey was ten times higher. But by a stroke of good fortune, the village of Langlade escaped the worst of the weather.

When Aurélien come back from Arles, having sold his honey, he sat down to work out his accounts. Having made his various calculations, he found that he still had a lot of money left over.

'A small fortune!' exclaimed the beekeeper.

Léopold counted the money again himself. He could hardly believe his eyes. Finally convinced, he turned to his grandson with a big grin on his face, and said:

'It would appear I owe you an apology, Aurélien. There is gold in honey after all! And if by chance, you were to get married now,' he added, trying to sound as if he meant nothing by it, 'well, what with the money from the lavender and that from the honey, we would have enough for a splendid wedding feast!'

It was obvious that the old man was thinking about Pauline. But Aurélien replied sadly:

'Summer is the time for weddings. And Summer has faded like the scent of the flowers. In any case, I'm going to use the money to build more hives. When I've finished what I started, perhaps then I may think about getting married. But for the time being, I'll give my love to the bees.'

13

Pauline thought of Aurélien as a bee that needed to go from flower to flower before finding the one that would offer him the most delicious of nectars.

She understood his restless nature, and his longing for gold. A longing that came with the warmth of the sun, and the lure of an elusive fragrance that drifted on the air.

And she had the patience to wait.

For she knew that in the end, a bee will always return to its hive.

Little by little, the beekeeper's dream was becoming a reality.

The day after his return from Arles, Aurélien hid his money under a loose stone in a corner of his workshop, and went out to catch butterflies. His favourite was called the 'Lemon of Provence' - a butterfly so yellow that it merged with the buttercups in the fields and looked like a splash of sunlight in the palm of his hand.

In the Autumn, Aurélien went mushroom-picking in the mountain above Langlade.

One morning, after torrential rain that had lasted all day and all night, he discovered a carpet of golden, yellow-cap mushrooms in a clearing strewn with wild myrtles. He picked enough to fill a whole basket.

That evening, while cleaning the mushrooms at the kitchen table, with the fire roaring in the fireplace, he found himself thinking of the life he was living.

And he felt truly happy.

But the day after that peaceful evening, everything changed.

He woke late that morning, gave a long yawn, and reluctantly got out of bed. He sipped his coffee while staring dreamily out of the kitchen window. The branches of the trees were stirring in the wind. The air was strangely warmer than the night before.

'The Foehn!' shouted Aurélien. 'The wind that drives people mad!'

Already the storm was approaching. Lightning flashed across the sky, and the thunder rumbled threateningly. Suddenly he heard Léopold's voice outside:

'Hurry! Aurélien! Hurry! The oak tree's on fire! It's been struck by lightning!'

Aurélien ran to the end of the garden, but the hives beside the burning tree were already on fire and the frantic bees were buzzing in and out of the hives. Léopold was trying in vain to put out the fire with a bucket.

'The hives!' shouted Aurélien. 'We must save the hives!'

He ran towards the well, coughing because of the smoke and began to haul up the bucket.

'Quick, Léopold! Quick! We must save the bees!'

The two men struggled for some time with the pulley, the buckets and the water, before realising it was too late. The fire had consumed everything in its path: the honey, the bees and the beehives too. It had turned the beekeeper's gold to a huge cloud of ashes that was spreading high in the sky.

All that was left of Aurélien's precious beehives was a pile of darkened wood and a heap of black-soaked ashes.

For a whole week, Aurélien locked himself away in his room. He was simply unable to come to terms with what had happened. Neither Léopold's words of comfort, nor Pauline's tenderness could help bring him out of his depression. The fire had taken away everything he cared about and he was weary even of life itself.

He lay on his bed for two days without even speaking. Then, on the morning of the third day, more for a change of scene than anything else, he went for a browse in his grandfather's library. He was staring aimlessly at the shelves, when the cover of one of the books caught his eye. He took it down from the shelf and began to read. The book was a novel set in Africa. It told the story of a man who had gone there in search of gold.

Hours later, having finished the book, Aurélien had an amazing dream, a dream that would change the course of his life.

In the dream, Aurélien found himself trudging through the desert when he reached the foot of a cliff down which a waterfall of clear, fresh water was cascading. Tired, and parched with thirst, he ducked beneath it, thrilled by the sudden contact of the water against his skin. He stood there delighting in the delicious coolness of the water flowing over his body.

After a while, he began to have the feeling that he was not alone and, as he turned round he saw a woman coming towards him. She was naked, and moved with a mysterious graceful beauty. Her hair and eyes were dark, but her skin was golden. Aurélien tried to speak to her but no sound would come from his mouth.

Slowly, the woman raised her hand, and as she did so, the waterfall changed from a torrent of white-flowing water, to a cascade of slow, golden honey.

The following day, the beekeeper went to find his grandfather.

'I'm going to look for gold,' he said, staring into his grandfather's blue eyes. He could see that the old man had not taken in what he had said.

'I'm leaving Laglande, leaving Provence. Leaving France.'

'But what about the bees?'

Aurélien didn't answer. He packed his bag and, after watching the fire crackling in the hearth, he decided it was time to leave.

'I'm going to look for gold,' he said again. 'In Africa.'

Then he swung the bag over his shoulder and off he went.

He turned to look back at the farmhouse for one last time. His grandfather had planted some lemon trees in front of the house. He found himself thinking of the Summer mornings he'd stood there, cupping a lemon in his hand, as the sun was rising across the fields. He stared at those fields now, and at the traces of ashes at the end of the garden that no one had had the heart to clear away.

Léopold followed him outside.

'But why gold?' he asked. 'Gold won't bring you the happiness you are seeking.'

Aurélien gave a long sigh, there was nothing more to say.

'What about the bees? You could start again. And there's always the lavender.'

'Please grandfather, just let me go.'

The old man stood there in silence, his blue eyes trying to fathom Aurélien's innermost thoughts. And what he saw chilled his heart. For there, in the young man's eyes, he saw a vast empty wilderness.

'You want to leave? Very well, then. I won't hold you back. But just tell me this: why Africa?'

'Because I had a dream and in the dream there was something about a woman and something about Africa.'

This wasn't the answer that Léopold was hoping to hear. But in the end there was nothing he could do. So he just stood there watching Aurélien's back as he walked off down the gravel path.

On his way, Aurélien stopped at the café where he sat down at a table to write a letter.

'What about Pauline?' said Clovis. 'If you leave, someone else will marry her.'

Aurélien waved him away, as if swatting some nagging doubt that he didn't want to deal with. It was Pauline he was writing to.

'If she really cares about me, she'll wait,' he said.

'But even if she does, what if you come back too late and find her already married?'

Aurélien smiled, calmly.

'In that case, she wasn't the one for me.'

21

When he saw her, Pauline was putting labels on her bottles of lavender. She was completely absorbed in what she was doing and applied each label delicately to the rounded surface of the glass.

Aurélien hesitated for a second, watching the young woman.

'I'm going away,' he said.

'Where to?'

'Africa.'

Aurélien paused, before going on.

'I'm going to look for gold.'

Pauline didn't bat an eyelid. She just kept her gaze fixed on the dark blue bottle that she held in her hands.

'There is gold here, too,' she said, sweetly. 'Gold in front of your very eyes, gold that you cannot see.' She spoke very softly, her voice betraying no trace of the emotions that raged within her.

But Aurélien wasn't listening, because for him the journey had already begun. And that was all he could think about now.

'Here, take this,' he said. 'I've written you a letter. I suppose it's what you might call a love letter.' His voice was so quiet it was barely more than a whisper.

'It's a letter that makes a promise,' he added. 'Don't open it until after I have gone.'

He gave her a white envelope inscribed in spidery black writing.

'Alright, Aurélien. Perhaps it is easier for us both that way. I'll read it later, when the bee has left his hive.'

She took the envelope and slipped it inside her blouse, where it rested against her quickening heart.

So Aurélien Rochefer found himself on the road to Marseilles, walking slowly towards the path of his dreams. Towards Abyssinia. In the book he had just finished reading, it said that Abyssinia was a place where a man could still make his fortune. A country so vast that huge regions of it were still undiscovered.

He didn't really know what he was going to find there, but he knew that his destiny was to look for something. Something the colour of the sun.

Passing through Arles, he stopped at the Hotel Carrel in rue Cavalerie.

As he was sitting on the terrace of the café, sipping his absinthe, he noticed a strange man painting in the street. The man was painting with an intensity that bordered on madness, and yet, despite his frantic movements, he did not make a sound. It was as if he was shut off from the rest of the world, sealed in a bubble of dreams. And inside that bubble, he was completely alone. He had red hair, he was wearing a straw hat and a lavender-blue shirt. His gaze was vague and distant.

As he got closer, Aurélien could see that the man was painting a self-portrait. He was painting without the aid of a mirror, but the likeness was amazing.

The curious thing was that to paint himself, the man was using a palette with so many colours: lemon yellow, pale green, ochre, emerald. In fact so many colours it made the mind dizzy just to look at the palette he was using.

'It's beautiful, so many different shades.'

The painter remained engrossed in his work as if he hadn't heard.

After a surprisingly long time, he looked at Aurélien and said:

'What do you know about colour?'

'Nothing.'

'So what do you want from me then?'

Aurélien was deeply embarrassed, but found himself saying:

'I'd like you to paint the portrait of a woman.'

The painter went on with his work.

'I don't have much money, but I have a bottle of lavender essence that I can give you in exchange.'

He opened his travelling bag and held up the blue glass bottle.

'When is she coming?'

'Who?'

'This woman I'm supposed to be painting.'

'Oh. She's not. She won't be coming.'

There was a long silence, during which the painter went on with his work.

'OK,' he said, finally turning his head. 'So how do you expect me to paint a portrait of a woman I don't even know?'

Aurélien saw that even his face was a riot of contrasting colours: a yellow and red beard, blue eyes, ginger hair.

'She is very beautiful and her skin is the colour of gold.'

The painter raised his eyebrows and said:

'Golden skin, you say?'

'Yes. That's all I know about her. You can imagine the rest for me.'

The artist thought that was a wonderful idea. To paint a woman who probably didn't even exist. But whose image was haunting this man.

He set up a new canvas on his easel, dabbed at the colours on his palette, and began to paint.

By evening, the painting was finished. The picture, and the bottle changed hands.

Aurélien looked at the painting, and saw a woman with black hair and black eyes, and skin the colour of gold.

'That's her,' he nodded.

'Thought so,' said the painter

Then saying goodbye, he packed up his things and went on his way.

Aurélien asked the landlord of the hotel to look after the painting while he was away.

'I'll pick it up on my way back. The name's Aurélien Rochefer. Don't forget.'

'When will you be coming back for it?'

The young man gave the briefest of smiles.

'If I knew that I wouldn't be going,' he said.

On Saint Céline's Day, Aurélien boarded a boat at the port of Marseilles bound for the Red Sea.

The crossing was slow and beautiful, the way only a sea-journey can be. They sailed first through the blue of the Mediterranean. Then came the coral reefs of the Red Sea. And, finally, the golden earth of Africa itself.

Aurélien celebrated his birthday alone. He was twenty-three, still only a young man. Yet, for the first time he had the feeling that his life was slipping away as if he had taken a sip from a poisoned cup. Though his sickness was not of the body but of the soul. For his soul felt incredibly heavy and, at the same time, wonderfully light, as if it had already travelled through several lifetimes. The one he was living now was the seventh. And the last.

As the waters of the Mediterranean slipped slowly along the side of the ship, Aurélien began to feel a strange uneasiness stealing over him. Wherever he looked, it was blue. A blue as hard and uncaring as fragments of flint, a blue as cold as the moon.

It was not until sunset, when the sun sank beneath the waves and turned the whole sea golden, that he felt at peace, once more.

The boat made its first port of call in Port-Said, where the sands of the desert merge with the sea. There was nothing to do there but wait.

Aurélien decided to visit the town. But finding himself pursued by beggars and then harassed by the merchants of the souk, he went back to the ship and didn't set foot ashore again.

That night he lay awake, listening to the barking of dogs which went on into the early hours. He went for a stroll up on deck, and was overcome by the sheer joy of being alive. He was at the place where two worlds meet. In his wake lay the calm blue waters of France, while ahead the Red Sea was almost in sight. He would soon be crossing the threshold of the East and be entering the very heart of the world.

1869 saw the opening of the Suez Canal. Thanks to the efforts of one Ferdinand de Lesseps, adventurers, travellers, and merchants now had a new route to Africa. At the time it had seemed like madness to allow the fire of the Red Sea to merge with the blue of the Mediterranean. But nineteen years later, Aurélien Rochefer was to take advantage of that madness.

As evening fell, the boat was gliding slowly through the waters of the Suez Canal, Aurélien stood watching the waves shaped by the opposing currents of two great seas. He could smell the fragrance of the East, the scent of spices and knew that now, at last, he was on the brink of Africa.

The ship docked at the port of Aden in the Yemen, and Aurélien stepped ashore. He had brought nothing with him. Nothing but his courage and his care-free nature.

Aden is a volcano. An enormous crater in a lunar landscape, where the earth is scorched by a thousand suns and pitted like the skin of an orange. The heat is suffocating, and the volcanic rock beneath the feet glows like an ember that refuses to go out.

Indeed as soon as he stepped ashore, Aurélien knew that he would not be staying long in that furnace. He looked South, where the rocks of Steamer Point were jutting out of the sea, and felt the urge to be on his way again. He had only one thought in his head: to cross the Red Sea and to go deeper into the heart of Africa.

He went up to the first group of men that he saw in the port.

'I have come here to look for gold,' he said. 'Where can I find a boat to cross the strait? I am trying to reach Harar.'

The men fell about laughing. One of them, a toothless old individual grinned through his rotten green gums.

'You'll find nothing in Africa,' he said, and spat a

dark ball of spittle on to the ground. 'Nothing but poverty, sickness and death. Go back where you came from. Unless you wish to die here.'

'That's the least of my worries,' said Aurélien, and with that he picked up his bag, nodded farewell, and began walking off into town.

The toothless old man understood that nothing he said would have any effect. He had seen it in his eyes. Aurélien was following a dream.

From Aden, there were two possibilities. One could either turn back, or cross the Red Sea. To stay there meant slowly being roasted alive.

Aurélien eventually fell in with a caravan of merchants. They were traders, and the loads that were piled on their camels contained oil and wax and weapons. They offered to take him with them, in exchange for a large sum of money.

'Where are you trying to get to?' they asked.

'I'm heading for the sacred City of Harar,' he said.

'Then come with us.'

So Aurélien joined the expedition.

There were seven men altogether including himself, all with skin burnt by the sun and scoured by the sandy wind, seven men riding their camels on a hazardous journey towards an unknown kingdom. Their leader was from the Yemen. His eyes were as black as the night itself, he had a scar running down half of his face, and wore a wicked-looking scimitar that never left his side. Drawn by the prospect of easy wealth, these men were on their way to sell their goods to the Chief of Harar.

That was, if they ever left. For each morning found them camped in the square where the camel market was held. It was there, sitting in front of Auguste Janvier's imposing residence that they waited in silence for the favourable moment to depart. Each morning the Yemenite chief met Aurélien with a gloomy expression and announced that the journey had been postponed.

'Why? What are we waiting for?'

'We're waiting for Janvier to pay us.'

Auguste Janvier was infamous.

He was extremely wealthy and owned the finest house in Aden.

He despised the locals and he hated women.

He was worth hundreds of pounds and several tons of gold.

But he was as mean in spirit as he was rich in money.

For three whole days the merchants remained camped outside Auguste Janvier's door.

'Auguste Janvier never pays,' said the leader.

'Why?' Aurélien asked him.

'Because he's rich. Those with money never pay. That's how they become rich.'

'How much does he owe you?'

'He owes us for one hundred kilos of coffee - a thousand thalers.'

'And as soon as you have this money the expedition can start?'

'Yes.'

The beekeeper looked thoughtful for a moment, and then said:

'Right, let's go and see this Monsieur Janvier.'

So the two men went to see Auguste Janvier. Being European, Aurélien had no difficulty gaining entry to the residence of the most influential merchant in the region.

Auguste Janvier was not expecting them. But then, Janvier was never expecting anyone. When they burst into his study, they came to face with a man of imposing stature who met them with a hard stare.

'Who gave you permission to come in here?'

'No-one,' said Aurélien. Then he gestured towards the Yemenite chief.

'Why won't you pay this man?'

Trembling from head to toe, the latter didn't say a word.

'I will pay him nothing. Because I owe him nothing. I deal only with civilised people. That coffee was stolen from some white trader, and I don't pay thieves.'

'In that case, it's me you owe the money to,' said Aurélien. 'This coffee belonged to me and I entrusted it to this man to sell on my behalf. So you owe me one thousand thalers.'

Auguste Janvier could barely conceal his amazement.

'You're lying,' he said staring at Aurélien.

'Prove it,' replied Aurélien. 'And try proving that you haven't just stolen the coffee yourself.'

Auguste Janvier smiled and took out a bundle of notes from his pocket.

'Here are five hundred thalers. Which is more than the coffee was worth, anyway. Now leave me be and give me your word that you will not meddle in the affairs of the locals again.'

Aurélien took the money, and handed it to the Yemenite chief. He moved towards the door, still holding Janvier's gaze.

'Don't worry,' he said, turning to go out of the room.

'My word is worth gold.'

34

In the square where the camel market was held, the Yemenites shouted with joy as the leader brandished the bundle of notes in front of them.

'How can I thank you?' asked the chief.

'By guiding me to the sacred city of Harar.'

'Consider it done. But is there nothing else I can do for you?'

'Just promise me that you'll never do business with that man again.'

35

They left Aden that evening. At nightfall they began loading the camels and their cargoes onto a boat. Aurélien was silent, content simply to take in the sights and sounds around him. What he saw was magical. The sleepy waters, the warm scented night, the coral sea. This was the real Africa. And there, visible at last across the waters that glistened in the starlight, was the land itself.

The following day, they arrived in Zeila where they turned away from the shores of the Red Sea and began to head into the Somali desert.

The real journey had begun.

The Somalian desert is a pitiless place, scorching during the day, and freezing at night. The wind never drops, there is no vegetation, and the stones underfoot are as sharp and as brittle as flint. Then there are snakes, scorpions, wild animals, and thirst to contend with, not to mention diseases, hostile tribes and, worst of all the sun. The implacable sun that shines unceasing from an empty sky.

That was the landscape through which the travellers would have to march for the next few weeks, despite the heat and the dangers it held. On the thirteenth day, one of the Yemenites was attacked by a wild animal and died from his wounds. A short while later, two men who were scouting ahead were killed by savage tribesmen. A fourth man, contracted dysentery, and died a few hours later. A fifth succumbed to malaria. Those that were left were forced to lighten their burdens by leaving behind some of their precious stores and to stagger on, exhausted.

The further they went into the desert, the more they had the feeling that they were fighting against the emptiness itself. Each day dawned like the one before, each time they broke camp was hell, each step they took brought pain.

For Aurélien, the Somalian desert was a terrifying initiation. For the first time in his existence, he could actually feel how precious life was. Here in the desert, life was dependent upon one thing: water. Water was the gold of the desert.

As the last drop of water dripped on to the beekeeper's tongue, the two men looked at each other, and knew that from now on, their lives depended on their ability to endure thirst.

'Harar is still two days march from here. We must keep going day and night. Otherwise we die here.'

Aurélien nodded his agreement. There was no sense wasting saliva by speaking.

Besides, he scarcely had any saliva left.

Thirst is a terrible ordeal. The pain of it can drive a man mad. That first day without water, Aurélien felt dizzy, he tried to concentrate on the landscape through which they were passing, but the aridness of the desert was now terrifying to him.

In the evening, when they stopped to rest for a while, he thought he would never get up again. Only the camels seemed able to endure the thirst.

'Do you think we'll make it?' he asked the Yemenite.

'We have to. Dying of thirst is one the most painful deaths imaginable. I've seen animals dying of thirst. It's a torture I would not wish on any human.'

Aurélien grew thoughtful for a moment.

'Do you think it's possible for a man to live seven lives?'

The Yemenite looked at him strangely. These were the words of a wise old sage, not those of a young European.

'I don't know. Perhaps some souls mature more slowly than others.'

'Seven is a good number. Seven life-times. And the seventh... is worth gold.'

The Yemenite nodded.

'And it is the last one that finally brings the treasure.'

There was a long silence, barely disturbed by the whispering of the wind.

'Well,' said Aurélien getting to his feet. 'It's time we got going.'

'Aren't you tired?'

The beekeeper ran his dry tongue across his thirst-cracked lips.

'I'm not tired of living.'

That night while they were walking through the desert, Aurélien had a realisation that normally only comes at the moment of death. Life is no more substantial than a thread. A golden thread woven from the days when one understands that the need to quench one's thirst will always be stronger than the pleasure of drinking. The need to stay alive will always be stronger than the joy of living.

And with every fibre of his being, he willed the thread not to break.

On the second day, the Yemenite chief found a few drops of dew that had collected on the stem of a plant.

'Here,' he said. 'There is little. But enough.'

Aurélien touched the water to his lips and those few drops of dew meant more to him than all the gold in the world.

'By nightfall we will be in Harar,' said the Yemenite.

'By nightfall we will be in Harar,' repeated Aurélien.

They did indeed arrive in Harar by nightfall. They had managed to overcome thirst, but they couldn't overcome their own kind.

As soon as they entered the city, they rushed to the nearest well and had only just quenched their thirst, when a group of armed men arrested them. They were brought before Chief Makonnen, the ruler of Harar.

Makonnen was sitting cross-legged on the floor, he was dressed very plainly in a sandy coloured tunic. His eyes were very black and lively, and he kept stroking his beard as he considered the two men before him.

'Who are you and what are you doing here?' he asked the Yemenite.

'I am a merchant. And I come to offer you oil, wax and weapons.'

He unpacked his goods. The Chief looked at them disdainfully.

'My land is rich in both oil and wax, so we have no need of those, and selling arms is forbidden here. Your goods will therefore be confiscated. You will be thrown out of the city for illicit business.'

The Yemenite protested loudly but two men took him away.

'And what about you?' the Chief asked, turning towards Aurélien.

'What have you come here for?'

'I'm looking for gold.'

'And that's the only reason you've come here, to Abyssinia?'

'It is.'

'You have been ill informed, my friend. You won't find anything of value here. All there is, is copper and clay. Any gold that this land may once have possessed, I have already taken for my own benefit. There is nothing left, not even a single nugget.'

'I'd still like to try my luck.'

'Do as you please. But first tell me this. Gold serves only one purpose. Do you know what it is?'

'It makes a man dream.'

Chief Makonnen was a god among men, and Aurélien Rochefer was a man among dreams. Just by looking at each other, both men realised that they were two of a kind. Each saw a brightness in the other's eyes. And the cause of that brightness was gold.

'You are free to wander at will throughout my territory,' said the Chief, 'as long as you respect the principles of Islam. Now go on your way!'

Aurélien thanked him and turned away. As he was nearing the door, his gaze met that of a young woman who was entering the room. She was so beautiful that he stopped in his tracks. Her hair had a soft black sheen and her skin was as golden as honey. The young woman passed by him without a word and went to bow in front of the Chief.

Before leaving the room, Aurélien turned back, and asked:

'Where should I go to find gold?'

Makonnen, who seemed to be expecting the question, answered while stroking his beard:

'There is no gold here, I've already told you that. It would be better for you to go back home.'

Aurélien looked at the Chief and then at the young woman by his side. For a brief moment she turned her head towards him. In that moment, he realised that there was something strangely familiar in her gaze.

Her glance was irresistible. Like a poison dart. He could feel it now, gripping his heart. And it throbbed like the sting of a bee.

The next day, Aurélien went back to the court. He knelt before the Chief.

'What is her name?' he asked.

Makonnen considered him a while before asking:

'Why are you interested in her?'

'Because she looks like a woman I have seen in my dreams.'

The Abyssinian started laughing.

'Dreams sometimes give bad counsel, my friend. You would do well to forget about her.'

And with that, he gestured for Aurélien to leave.

44

The following day, still unable to get the young woman out of his head, Aurélien returned to see Makonnen.

'Who is she?'

'I don't know. As a matter of fact, nobody knows who she is. The young Gala women are very mysterious.'

'Even if you can't tell me her name, can you at least tell me where I can find her?'

Again the Chief's answer was evasive:

'No one knows. She will have gone back to her village by now, up in the mountains.'

'Which mountains?'

The Chief made a vague gesture, as if he was swatting at a fly. It was clear that the audience was over.

Aurélien sighed, and rose to his feet.

On the fourth day, Aurélien went back to the palace again and, as before, he knelt down in front of the Chief and asked him:

'Who is this woman?'

'You are as stubborn as a donkey. I've already told you. She is a young Gala woman.'

'Where is she now?'

This time the Chief didn't answer.

Aurélien stood up and was getting ready to leave, convinced once again that his question would remain unanswered. Then, while slowly stroking his beard, the Chief said:

'This is the third time you've asked me the same question and, according to our custom, it is forbidden to lie three times in a row. So here is the answer to your question: if you find the Land of the Bees, you will find what you are looking for.'

The voice of the Abyssinian had rung out like the prayer-call of a muezzin thrown from the height of a minaret. After a long silence, as if he was about to reveal a secret only known to the gods, Aurélien repeated in a very low voice: 'The Land of the Bees?'

'Yes. A mountain with its sides stacked with beehives filled with honey. We call this place the Land of the Bees. And according to legend, there is more honey there than in the whole of Abyssinia.'

At first, Rochefer couldn't tell whether Makonnen was telling the truth or if he was lying in order to scare him away. But when the Chief looked him straight in the eye, Aurélien realised that he was trying to help him.

'Where will I find this place?'

'It is in the high country. In the land of the Gala.'

Makonnen silently smoothed his beard. He picked up an orange and began to tear into it with his teeth. The juice spurted on to his hand and three golden droplets fell on to the bare earth, each one raising a tiny cloud of dust.

'I will go there,' Aurélien said. 'And I will find this woman.'

'Do not forget that the Land of the Bees is a sacred place.'

'So why have you told me about it?'

'Nothing can stop you from following your dream. But you should know this: if you enter the Land of the Bees, you will be breaking the law of the Gala people, and in doing so, you will be risking your life.'

Aurélien became thoughtful for a moment, his fingers stroking an imaginary beard.

'That is a risk I am willing to take.'

On the fifth day, it was Makonnen who sent for Aurélien.

'The journey, you are about to undertake is a dangerous one,' the Chief said. 'I have the feeling that you will find what you are looking for, and then regret having found it. Why not go back to Aden and return to your country?'

'Because what I need can only be found in Africa.'

The Chief bowed his head in acknowledgement. He beckoned one of his servants and gave him an order. After a few minutes, the man returned with a silver box which he presented to Aurélien.

'Open it,' said the Chief.

Aurélien lifted the lid and inside were two small bees, made out of the purest gold.

'These are for you,' said Makonnen. 'When you look at them, you will remember me, and your dream, and Africa.'

A week later, Aurélien Rochefer left the city of Harar in search of the Land of the Bees.

As it was dangerous to travel alone, he joined an expedition bound for Ankober. They were going to sell arms to King Menelik. The expedition consisted of five men, and was led by a Frenchman who the others referred to as the Faranji.

'Who are you?' he asked Aurélien. 'And were are you going?'

'I'm looking for gold and my destination lies seven days march west of Harar.'

'You may journey with us,' he said. 'It will cost you fifty thalers, and you must bring your own food.'

Aurélien paid the money and the leader of the expedition stuffed it into his belt.

The expedition left and, for the rest of the day, none of the men spoke a word. At nightfall, they stopped by a well to rest.

After eating around the fire, the Faranji finally broke his silence:

'There is no gold in those mountains. What are you really going there for?'

Aurélien knew it would be unwise to tell this man anything other than the truth. He took a cigarette from his pouch, which he lit with a piece of glowing wood from the fire. He drew on it slowly and, while exhaling the smoke, he answered:

'I'm looking for the Land of the Bees.'

The Faranji stared at him with his small sparkling eyes.

'An old man told me of it once. But that was a long time ago. I don't even know if the place really exists. Where did you hear about it?'

'In a dream.'

The Faranji lifted his eyes towards the sky and stared at the stars for a while.

'Well, if you saw it in a dream, it might be worth looking for.'

After they had been travelling for two days, the expedition stopped near an oasis where the camels could drink. The men ate and then laid out their mats and went to sleep.

The Faranji filled a small clay pipe with tobacco and began to smoke. Aurélien sat down beside him.

'What were you doing in France?' asked Rochefer.

'I was bored.'

'And that was why you came to Africa?'

'Yes. But nowadays I'm just as bored here. I must be cursed. I'd like to go back home and get married. But without money, who would want me?'

Aurélien didn't answer.

'What about you? What were you doing?'

'I was a beekeeper.'

'So that's why you're looking for the Land of the Bees?'

'No. Originally I came here to look for gold. And then by chance I saw a woman I'd seen in a dream. So now here I am, searching for the Land of the Bees. One coincidence has led to another.'

'There is no such thing as coincidence,' said the Faranji. Then he blew a puff of white smoke that drifted slowly towards the golden blanket of stars.

In the morning, when he opened his eyes, Aurélien felt something moving beneath his blanket.

'Don't get up,' said the Faranji. 'Turn on your side, very slowly.'

Aurélien did as he was told. When he had turned over in the sand, he saw that he had been sleeping on a scorpion's nest.

'Scorpions are always drawn towards warmth. Especially at night, when it's cold. You'll know that from now on.'

The beekeeper thanked him.

'Don't thank me. Thank the desert. For showing you how to stay alive.'

For the next few days, they journeyed on in silence. It was too hot even to talk.

On the sixth day, they came across a group of Gala people going to the market in Harar to sell some sheep. The Faranji asked them the way to the Land of the Bees. They answered in their own dialect and then went on their way.

'It is not far away now,' he said to Aurélien. He pointed across the desert towards a range of mountains standing out against the horizon like a quietly shimmering mirage.

'You see that mountain,' he said to Aurélien, 'Well somewhere, the other side of that, your destiny awaits you.'

'What about you, Faranji? Where will you be going?'

The man turned his thin face to the sky. For a second it seemed as if he was transfixed by a ray of sunlight.

'My path lies over that way,' he said, 'but I'm still not sure where it leads.'

The Land of the Bees was high in the mountains, in one of the most remote parts of the Gala territory. The expedition reached it towards evening on the seventh day after they'd set out from Harar. It was a place so remote that it seemed to be cut off from the rest of the world. The air was fresh and the slopes were covered in luxuriant vegetation. The landscape was breathtaking.

The Faranji left Aurélien Rochefer the same evening, pointing towards a path that led upwards, disappearing into the mountain, between two rocky slopes.

'It is time for us to go our separate ways. Good luck to you, Mr Beekeeper.'

'Good luck to you, too.'

The expedition took the road for Ankober, and the Faranji disappeared from view behind a rock.

Aurélien was alone. Alone with the wind and the rocks, and the desert. Yet he felt no fear. In this solitude he felt at one with the desert. He took a deep breath. The red horizon stretched as far as the eye could see. He was alone in the middle of the desert and that made him feel powerful. Everything around him was a part of himself. Even the silence. Standing facing the sun, he experienced the joy of living.

He walked for miles across stones as sharp as knives, until he reached a plateau with a sheer drop on three sides, bordered to the north by a steep rockface. He appeared to have reached an impasse. He thought about trying to scale the cliff-face itself, hoping to find a path to continue his ascent, but the wall of rock was impassable.

He was about to retrace his steps when he thought he heard something. He listened carefully. It sounded like water. It was water. Here in the middle of the desert, he had discovered a spring.

52

The spring poured out of the rock as if by magic.
It had been flowing since the beginning of time.
Water coming from nowhere.

And yet there it was, a miracle in the middle of
the desert.

It was there, it was real. It was a living thing.

53

Aurélien knelt down and began to drink. Having quenched his thirst, he got up and started following the course of the stream among the rocks.

It was then that another sound reached his ears. A music, more vibrant than the quiet flowing song of the water. Aurélien lifted his head to look at the cliff and saw that he had reached the end of his journey.

There above him was the Land of the Bees.

Myriads of bees were flying above him. Their buzzing was so loud it was almost deafening. The rockface was home to millions of bees. Flecks of moving gold against the warm black rock. Above them, so high up as to be almost indistinguishable from the rockface itself there were figures moving about.

These were the honey gatherers. Dangling from a rope ladder, one of them was trying to coax a swarm from a crevice in the rock. With the aid of a stick, he pierced the wax that sealed the surface and allowed the honey to drip into a jar. Like fusing gold, the honey seeped from the black rock.

While three men carefully hauled the pot full of honey to the top of the cliff, the honey gatherer went down the rope ladder with impressive agility. When he reached the ground, he took off the cloth that was protecting his face.

And to his surprise Aurélien saw that it was a woman.

55

She was beautiful. And she was watching him. She let slip the stiff canvas robe that she had been wearing to protect her from the stings of the bees. Beneath it, she was naked, except for a golden triangle covering her sex.

She dipped her hand inside the jar and crushed the wax between her fingers to squeeze out the honey. Ever so slowly, she brought her hand to her mouth. Aurélien watched the gold trickle down her skin and felt a shiver of pleasure.

After that, the young woman went to bathe herself in the torrent of water running down from the cliff. Then she went towards Aurélien, took his hand in hers and without saying a word, she led him towards the village.

'I've come here to look for gold,' Aurélien said.

But the young woman couldn't understand his strange words and each time he opened his mouth to speak, she would only laugh.

The village appeared to be no more than a temporary encampment. It had been built against the rock on the south side of the plateau, and in order to reach it, one had to lean right out over the edge of the precipice. The mud huts were arranged next to each other like the cells of a beehive. In the centre, surrounded by the others was the hut belonging to the Queen - the woman with the golden skin, whom he had first seen at the court of Chief Makonnen. It was in this hut he was left to wait for her. It was clear to Aurélien that she was a woman of great power, and she ruled over both the men as well as the women of the tribe.

When she arrived, Aurélien was sitting cross-legged in the middle of the hut. She stood over him, staring into his eyes. Then she clapped her hands. Two men came in bearing a large bowl of fruit, a jug of water and a jar full of honey.

She took a piece of fruit in her hand, dipped it into

the honey and brought it teasingly to her lips. A drop of honey dripped from the side of her mouth to her neck and very slowly down on to her naked breast. Aurélien swallowed, unable to take his eyes off the progress of that single drop of honey. He raised his head and looked into two black eyes gloating with pleasure.

The woman smiled, took another piece of fruit, dipped it into the honey and, held it up to his mouth. Aurélien let her feed him, like a child. And as he tasted the fruit, he felt a strange sweetness flooding through his body.

That evening, the tribe held a feast in his honour. Aurélien was given bowls of fruit, royal jelly and nectar. The drums played a hypnotic rhythm and the women danced around the fire.

The queen watched the spectacle in silence, occasionally clapping her hands to the rhythm of the music. She sat cross-legged in front of the fire, with Aurélien beside her. They ate without ever looking at each other. After the meal the queen took the foreigner by the hand and led him into her hut.

That night, while the feast went on outside, she made love to him, and all the time they lay together she seemed to be devouring him with her black eyes.

Aurélien, unable to see anything but those two flames glowing in the shadow of the darkened hut, allowed himself to be slowly overcome by the sheer joy of being alive.

58

In the morning, Aurélien woke up, as if emerging from a beautiful dream.

He rubbed his eyes, and looked about him. The dream came flooding back. He got up from his bed. The woman with the golden skin was gone.

Outside the hut, the sun was already high in the sky, and a heavy silence hung over the village. He was completely alone.

The honey-gatherers had gone. On the rockface where he'd first seen them, the bees were still collecting the nectar and storing their honey into the black rock. But the men and their queen had disappeared.

Their behaviour was like that of the bees. After making love to him, the queen had vanished. The woman with the golden skin had abandoned him.

59

Aurélien went back to the hut and there on his bag was a golden bee. A bee carved from a single nugget of gold. He picked it up and, after looking at it for a while, he slipped it into the pocket of his shirt.

He looked over the silent, deserted village for the last time. Then he stepped through the veil that was his dream and returned to the world of reality.

Aurélien Rochefer wandered the high Abyssinian plateaus for many weeks. But he never saw the tribe of the bees nor their Queen again. Neither did he see any sign of the gold he had gone there to find. None, except the memory of a single drop of honey, and the taste of that sun-darkened skin.

Aurélien Rochefer returned to Harar and went straight to the court of Makonnen. When the Chief saw him, he couldn't hide his surprise.

He gestured to the young man to sit down in front of him and ordered his courtiers to leave them in peace.

Rochefer immediately asked the question that was burning on his lips:

'Where is she?'

'I never thought to see you again,' the Chief replied.

The silence hung between them.

'So you managed to find her, then. And I can tell from your eyes that you made love to her, too. I could see that as soon as you entered the room.'

'Where is she now?' Aurélien repeated.

'Nobody knows. Most of the time the tribe are never seen. Once a year they go to the rockface to gather the honey. Then they vanish again.'

There was another silence. Even longer than the one before.

'If there was any way of finding her, I'd go back there right away.'

'That would be unwise,' said Makonnen shaking his

head. 'The woman with the golden skin shares only one night with her lovers. To share her bed more than once means certain death.'

Aurélien realised that what the Chief was saying made sense, that by leaving him behind, the queen had saved his life.

'And the golden bee?'

Aurélien took it out of his pocket and showed it to him.

'You will never forget this woman as long as you live,' the Chief told him.

And with that, Aurélien passed through the doors and did not return.

II

One morning, with the sun red behind them, a convoy entered the city of Aden. Among the travellers was a man named Aurélien Rochefer. He had just spent the last few months in the desert of Abyssinia.

His body was covered in a fine layer of dust and beneath it his skin was the colour of honey.

He left the convoy and walked towards a well where he drank the water which tasted of bitter oranges. In the freshness of dawn, he watched the stars disappearing one by one in the eastern sky. He had walked hundreds of miles before coming back here, to Aden, and this long trek by the light of the moon had left him exhausted. He spread a mat on the sand and fell asleep in the shadow of a palm tree.

When he woke up, the sun was high overhead. Some veiled women were drawing water from the well. Aurélien went over and asked where he could find the English quarter. He said he wanted to talk to the British Consul. He had spoken in their language but none of the women answered. Some just smiled, while others started giggling and pointing at him. With his clothes plastered with sweat, and his face caked with sand, they

had mistaken him for a beggar. But the youngest of them could see that his features were European.

'The man you are looking for lives by the South Gate of the City,' she said to Aurélien. 'The consulate is a big white building. But you can't go and see him looking like that.'

The young girl had a big terracotta jug in her hands. She tipped it up and poured the water slowly on the foreigner's hair. Aurélien shivered as the water splashed over him. When the jug was empty, he turned towards her and said simply:

'Thank you.'

Then he rummaged inside his bag and took out the silver box the Chief had given him, the one containing the three golden bees. He gave one to the young girl. She looked at him in astonishment.

'This is for you. It will bring you luck.'

'But what I have told you is not worth as much as this. I can't accept such a treasure.'

She tried to give it back to him but Aurélien closed the young girl's hand on the bee.

'It wasn't only what you told me. You gave me water when I was thirsty and, more than that, you spoke to me while the others just laughed.'

The young girl lowered her gaze on the metal that was shining on the palm of her hand. She then stared at the foreigner and asked:

'Who are you? And where have you come from?'

Aurélien sighed. His blond hair, still wet, was even brighter than the sun, but his heart was heavy.

'I am a dream,' he murmured. 'And I come from a dream.'

He stood there in silence and then he added:

'A dream to which I have lost the key.'

Aurélien headed towards the southern gate. He wandered the narrow streets trying to find his way. Nobody so much as looked at him. A couple of times, someone bumped into him but without ever meeting his gaze. He seemed to have become invisible to them all.

When he arrived at the English consulate, he requested an audience. An old servant made him wait in a room that overlooked the street. The noise of the city seemed to him like a repetitive chant made unbearable by the incredible heat that rose from the ground. When the Consul received him in his office, he was taken aback by his youth and by his bearing. What was this man doing, lost, in Aden? And what was he doing alone? Judging from his lost gaze, this man must have been wandering around Africa for some time.

'Forgive my indiscretion, Sir, but might I ask you where you have come from?'

'I've come from Abyssinia, from the city of Harar to be precise.'

The Consul flinched. This man had come from a very unfriendly region where even the most daring explorers would be risking their lives.

'Harar is a dangerous place. The road there is long and perilous, most people who go there never return.'

'I found that out for myself. It took me three years to leave Abyssinia.'

'Three years in Abyssinia? I must say I find that incredible.'

'And yet it is the truth.'

'What have you been doing there for three years?'

'I've been dreaming.'

Aurélien drew his hand slowly across his forehead and massaged the back of his neck. The heat was suffocating. The Consul couldn't decide whether this man was telling the truth, but it was obvious that he was almost collapsing with exhaustion.

'And besides this dream, what were you looking for there?'

Aurélien didn't answer.

'Please forgive my curiosity, but it is not often I have the opportunity to speak with someone who has survived the journey you have undertaken.'

'I was looking for gold.'

The Consul stood up and crossed the room. He stood in front of the window contemplating the ever-restless city of Aden. Then he turned towards Aurélien and said:

'Either you were trying to find gold, or you were trying to find yourself.'

Then, he seemed to regret what he had just said, and

added: 'Though from the look of you, I should say that your search is not yet over.'

Aurélien could see there was no point trying to tell his story to this man. What could he possibly know of Abyssinia and the young Gala woman, when he was stuck here in this office? What could he understand of the Land of the Bees and the years of wandering that followed? He kept quiet and just nodded agreement as the Consul went on with his monologue.

'You are not the first. Many have passed through here, travellers in search of the absolute, those seekers of gold who are really looking for a reason for living. I can tell them as soon as I seen them. They come back, poorer than before, their illusions shattered. Anyway, Sir, what can I do for you?'

The young man squinted at the harsh light that came through the slats of the blinds.

'I'd like you to help me return home.'

During the return journey from Aden to Marseilles, Aurélien fell ill with dysentery. He was in great pain and for him the crossing was an ordeal. His only comfort during the trip was the fact that he made the acquaintance of an eccentric individual by the name of Hippolyte Loiseul. He was an engineer by profession and had been working on some important projects for the Sultan of Tunis.

Like the painter he'd met all those years before in Arles, Hippolyte Loiseul was an unusual man to say the least, and Aurélien would have found it very difficult to choose one colour to describe him.

When he spoke, he shouted. When he laughed, the glass in his hand would tremble. And when he smoked, his voice would emerge from an indescribable fog. But what he did best was talk, and he would hold forth about every subject under the sun.

While Aurélien was ill, Hippolyte would stay by his bedside and tell him about his trips, his projects and his crazy dreams.

Aurélien would listen in silence. He'd shut his eyes and drift off to faraway places, lulled by the sound of the man's voice.

'It's true,' he would say, 'I was a king there in Africa. I built the first road from Carthage to the Sahara desert. And on my travels I've met a thousand women.'

'I met only one,' replied Aurélien. 'Her skin was the colour of honey. And she was looking after bees.'

The secret had slipped out. But the Gala woman was far away now, and even if she could have heard him it wouldn't have bothered her. He took out the two golden bees and showed them to Loiseul. Suddenly, the engineer stopped talking. Then, slowly, he lit a cigar, puffed on it and said:

'Tell me about her, and about the bees.'

65

By the time Aurélien had finished his story, the two men had the feeling that a rare and precious friendship was just beginning.

'It is a beautiful story. A most beautiful story.'

'I can't stop dreaming about this woman. I don't know how to find her again, or how to forget her.'

After a long pause, the engineer said:

'There is no need to forget anything. Come and see me in Paris. Perhaps I can help you realise your dream.'

'I don't know if I'll have the strength to come to Paris.'

'In that case, I shall come and visit you in Langlade. As soon as I can. Because, when someone has a dream like yours, it is important to make it come true as soon as possible, before the tides of life carry it away.'

In September 1891, Aurélien arrived in Marseille and was admitted to the hospital of the Immaculate Conception.

Hippolyte Loiseul accompanied him there, then receiving an urgent summons, he went back to Paris.

'You'll be up and about in a fortnight,' he told Aurélien as he was saying goodbye.

In fact it took two months for Rochefer to get better. Two months of pain and boredom during which he had plenty of time to reflect.

When he felt strong enough to walk, he took to wandering the hospital corridors in order to pass the time. In the room next to his, was a man who had had his leg amputated. He was delirious, and kept muttering disjointed phrases about Africa, the desert, and Abyssinia. Hanging from the bedpost was a belt full of gold.

'Faranji!' shouted Aurélien going to his bedside. 'Do you remember me?'

But the man didn't seem to recognise him.

'Who are you?' he asked, his eyes wide with delirium.

'I am Aurélien Rochefer. We travelled together in Abyssinia. Don't you remember me?'

'Perhaps. I'm not sure anymore.'

The Faranji couldn't remember anything. Nothing mattered to him anymore. Neither his own impending death, nor anybody else's.

Shortly before he died, the Faranji gave Aurélien a small collection of poems he had written.

'Take it, they are all that is left. All that is left of me.'

Aurélien eagerly read the poems. Then, almost in tears, he said:

'They are beautiful. Very beautiful.'

'Fragments. Nothing but fragments,' said the Faranji. 'But they justify everything else, all the suffering.'

Aurélien asked him one final question:

'Have you been happy?'

But he received no answer.

67

On his way back home, Aurélien Rochefer stopped in Arles, at the Hotel Carrel.

He asked about the painter. The man who three years earlier had painted the portrait of the woman with the golden skin in exchange for a bottle of lavender.

He was told that the painter had vanished without trace, evaporated like the scent of the lavender, but the canvas he had painted that day was still in the cellar.

'Can I see it?' asked Aurélien. 'And perhaps could I have a glass of absinthe. I've been dreaming about it for the past three years.'

'About seeing the painting again or about drinking a glass of absinthe?' asked the hotel owner.

'Both.'

He sent his wife to look for the painting while he poured the absinthe. One glass, then another, thinking that, after all this time, Aurélien must have been very thirsty.

The woman came back carrying a small painting. It was a golden yellow colour, with a spot of blue for the sun. He contemplated the canvas and realised that he was admiring a masterpiece.

'There it is. It really is her. That man was a genius.'

Without taking his eyes off the canvas, Aurélien asked the hotel owner:

'So this painter, do you have any idea what happened to him?'

The man shrugged while drying the counter.

'I don't know. He left as he came. He may even be dead by now for all I know.'

Aurélien paid for his drinks and was getting ready to leave. As he put the canvas away in his case, he looked at it once more. The woman with the golden skin.

'A masterpiece. A true masterpiece,' he kept repeating to himself.

'Do you think he was happy with his life?' he asked on his way out.

But, this time, he didn't wait for the answer.

'Wonderful – so you're back at last!' Léopold's voice greeted the traveller. He had received a telegram from Marseille and he had gone to the station in Arles to welcome Aurélien. He was standing on the platform, leaning on his cane, a sprig of lavender in his hand.

Aurélien threw himself into his arms and hugged him. He took the sprig of lavender and sniffed it.

'I've never forgotten this scent.'

'How could you ever forget it? said Léopold.

The young man put the lavender away in his pocket, put his hand on his grandfather's shoulder and gave him a big smile.

Back in Langlade, Clovis welcomed them in his usual jovial way.

'Here he is! The traveller returns!'

After many hugs during which Clovis cried a lot and poured glass after glass of absinthe, Léopold and Aurélien headed home.

'So, in the end, all that travelling was for nothing?'

'Not at all, grandfather. Not at all. It has left me with scents, images and many memories.'

'And what have you been doing all this time?'

'Well, I've grown a little older.'

A pause.

'And I've brought this back.'

He gave him the small box containing the two golden bees.

'What is it?'

'It is the fortune I went there to find.'

'I have a plan!'

'That's the second time you've told me that,' he said. 'And the first time it ended badly.'

Aurélien looked at his grandfather and began to smile.

'Anyway, what's been happening here? How's life?'

'Well you know… here in the village things haven't changed that much while you've been away. Time seems to pass more slowly here than elsewhere. It's as if the hourglass was blocked, and a grain of sand has become lodged in the stem and prevents the time from flowing freely.'

'A grain of sand as big as a nugget?' asked Aurélien.

'A nugget eh? So did you find that gold after all?'

'No, but I've been thinking…'

'Will you go back to beekeeping?'

'Well, I want to be a beekeeper again. But I'll do things differently this time.'

'After all that's happened? But that's crazy!'

'Well you see, the first time I didn't know which path to follow. Now I know for certain. I am Aurélien Rochefer, and I have come back from Africa. With a purpose to fulfil.'

Aurélien turned towards the old man and added:
'Do you know what I'm going to do here?'
'No.'
'Something beautiful.'

The following day he went to see Pauline.

'You're back,' she said simply, as if he'd only left the night before.

'Yes. I came back. For the bees.'

He showed her the two golden bees and explained his project to her.

Pauline bit her lips. She was almost in tears, but he was so caught up in his dreams that he didn't even notice.

'I'm going to start again. But this time everyone will be astounded. It will be so beautiful that you won't believe it.'

A shadow crept across Pauline's face but he went on, oblivious.

'You know, I had an amazing experience over there,' he said.

'I'm happy for you.'

Pauline turned away so as to hide her feelings. Then unable to contain herself, she added:

'She must be beautiful, the woman of your dreams!'

She took a letter from among the lavender bottles and gave it to Aurélien.

'I think you better have this back.'
'Why? Isn't it a beautiful love letter?'
Pauline sighed:
'Yes. Very beautiful. But it wasn't for me.'

In Langlade, Aurélien Rochefer went back to beekeeping, carefully tending his thirty new hives. The harvest of 1892 was good and the beekeeper slowly started to enjoy his first love again.

When the snow arrived, the bees started to hibernate in the warmth of their hives. There was enough honey on the shelves to last until Spring.

One morning, while Aurélien was attending his bees, Léopold went to see him. He sat down on a stump covered with snow, took his hat off and said:

'What happened in Africa?'

Aurélien pretended not to hear him.

'Tell me what happened!'

'Nothing very interesting. I looked for gold and I found honey. That's it.'

'I'm not talking about honey, I'm talking about love. You met a woman, I'm sure of it!'

The beekeeper turned to face his grandfather.

'Who told you about a woman?'

'Nobody told me. Least of all yourself. I just know.'

That Winter, life seemed sweet to the beekeeper, while he waited patiently for the coming of Spring.

When the weather was fine, Aurélien began to prepare for his second season. He was happy. Happy and serene. As a matter of fact, he was on the verge of beginning his new project. All he was waiting for was a letter.

A letter from Hippolyte Loiseul.

The letter finally arrived in April 1893. Having spent the morning looking after his beehives, Aurélien went to see Clovis to quench his thirst.

It was there that the postman found him, sitting in the sun, with Clovis and two glasses of absinthe.

'Just enough water to cloud the absinthe,' Clovis said again.

The postman handed Aurélien Hippolyte Loiseul's letter. This seemed to bring the Summer even closer. It was a letter filled with the joys of life. A letter that announced the arrival of the engineer on the first of May.

The day of the flowers.

'And what sort of a person is your engineer?'

'He's one of a kind.'

'What else?'

'He's not coming on his own. He's bringing what I'm missing.'

Clovis scratched his head and frowned: 'He's bringing a woman?'

'No. He's bringing money.'

Hippolyte Loiseul was an engineer so knowledgeable and so inquisitive that he was fascinated by all the marvels of the natural world. He was most interested in the *hymenopterae*, more specifically bees and in particular, the *apis mellifica*. And he never forgot a promise.

He arrived in Langlade on the morning of the first of May 1893. Aurélien was busy looking after his beehives and so it was Léopold who welcomed him.

The two men were soon sitting outside the Green Cabaret, where Loiseul was puffing away on one of those enormous cigars that can be found only in Havana.

'So what were you doing in Africa?' Léopold asked the rather corpulent figure opposite him.

'The same as your nephew,' he replied.

'You were looking for gold too?'

'You could put it like that. But I have found it!' roared Loiseul.

He took a long puff from his cigar and exhaled a big cloud of white smoke that disappeared among the leaves of an olive tree.

'Do you want to know how?'

Léopold nodded.

'By making dreams come true.'

'Dreams?'

'Yes, as simple as that. Everyone has a secret dream but, most of the time, they don't have the courage to realise it. And this is when Hippolyte Loiseul steps in. And do you know what the purpose of realising someone else's dreams is?'

'I don't know… to bring people closer together?'

'No. To obtain gold.'

A long silence.

'What do you want from Aurélien?'

'To help him.'

'How?'

'When we first met, he told me about his time as a beekeeper, and about his experiences, over in Africa. So I have come here to talk with him about bees. And above all,' he said waving his cigar under Léopold's nose, 'I will help him find the gold he is looking for. I will help bring his plan into being.'

'What plan?'

'Hasn't he told you?'

'No.'

Hippolyte Loiseul began to laugh, and his laugh made the glasses on the table rattle. Opening his arms as if to wrap the sky and all the fields around, he rolled his eyes gleefully and bellowed at the top of his voice:

'I'm going to help him create Apipolis! The land of the bees!'

Because, for Aurélien's bees, as with everything in his life, Hippolyte Loiseul had great plans.

Hippolyte Loiseul had a secret ambition: he wanted to become famous. He wanted his name to be remembered by future generations. Each night, as he was drifting to sleep, he would imagine his statue in front of the town hall in Paris. A statue with the dedication:

To Hippolyte Loiseul
Engineer
in gratitude.

And the engineer was finally ready to make this secret dream come true.

That night, Hippolyte Loiseul took a room in the Green Cabaret.

'I'm sorry it's not a green room,' said Clovis, 'but it's the only one I have left.'

In fact the room had blue wallpaper and the curtains were a deep lavender colour. Hippolyte settled down so well that his snoring was soon heard throughout the whole hotel.

The next day at dawn he had his breakfast at the café. To Clovis' pleasure, and his wife's distress, he had a glass of orange juice, three cups of tea, seven pieces of toast with honey, four eggs and a whole pot of jam.

'He is what I call a good customer!'

Then, with a full stomach, he put a straw hat on his head, took up his cane, lit an enormous cigar and ambled off towards the Rochefer's farmhouse.

'And how are we going to set about creating Apipolis?'

'Using this!'

Aurélien looked at the manual that the engineer was brandishing in his hand.

'A book?' he said, doubtfully.

'Yes Aurélien, a book. A book that is going to make your fortune. Don't forget: all books come from dreams, and all dreams come from books.'

Hippolyte had not simply come to Langlade with the idea of creating an extraordinary colony of several million bees that would pollinate the most beautiful flowers in France and produce the finest lavender honey in the world. He had come with a complete treatise on the project, a work with plans, technical notes, forecasts and all kinds of charts to explain the art and the way to realise a dream of the scale of Apipolis.

'And who wrote this book?' asked Aurélien.

Hippolyte stood up and, patting his chest, he said:

'Why, me of course! Who else?'

Because besides being an engineer, Hippolyte Loiseul was a botanist, a geologist, a mathematician, a writer and a scientist. In short, a man who knew all kinds of things. For whenever he became interested in a subject, he would study it voraciously. He would read everything he could get his hands on. He would meet all the experts, the most eminent scientists from all over the world. And, after a certain period of time, which could be anything from a month to several years, he would write a book on the chosen subject. A book that, even if it was rarely considered authoritative on the matter, was in any case authoritative for him.

Aurélien leafed through the book and was startled to discover that according to Loiseul's forecasts, Apipolis would produce more than twenty thousand kilos of honey in the first year alone and, once the costs and salaries were deducted, that would result in a net profit of thirty thousand gold francs.

'But how can I reach such an astronomical figure with my thirty-seven beehives?'

'Well firstly,' replied Hippolyte, 'we are not talking about thirty-seven beehives but a thousand! And secondly, you need a whole rockface covered in beehives, like the one you saw in Africa! With a thousand queen bees! And ten honey gatherers to collect the honey!'

'But where are we going to get the money we need for all of this? Not to mention the hundreds of thousands of bees we'd need to produce all this honey?

How are we going to get everything?'

Hippolyte took a thick bag out of his pocket and opening it said:

'With this!'

In the bag there were ten thousand gold francs.

'This should be enough for the first couple of seasons,' said Hippolyte.

In fact the money lasted less than three months. Because although Loiseul and Aurélien with their crazy dreams were mere humans, their vision of Apipolis was a project on an almost divine scale.

'First, we have to mark out the area of the rockface we are going to use, and then we can begin setting up the building site,' said the engineer.

'What building site?'

'Call it what you like. Apipolis. The Doomed Rock. Bee View. But it will be a building site until Autumn. And people will still be talking about it in a thousand years!'

He put his hand on Aurélien's shoulder and added:

'And then I'll get my statue!'

The construction of Apipolis was carried out under the watchful eye of the engineer himself. He was a man with the appearance of a mad genius, the ability of a diplomat and the virtuosity of an orchestral conductor.

For the site, Loiseul had chosen a steep chalky cliff fifty feet high and a hundred wide not far from the Rochefer farmhouse.

'It is perfect,' he said. 'There's even a mule path leading up to the top.'

'Why would you want to go climbing up there?' asked Aurélien.

'It won't just be me going up there. We need to get all the building materials up there too.'

'And how are you proposing to do that?'

The engineer furrowed his brow.

'Well it's a mule path. What's the best way of getting things up a mule path?'

So they rented a mule from the local miller to carry everything up to the top. Then they ordered several hundred wicker beehives from a couple of gypsies coming from the Camargue, together with some rope and a basket strong enough to withstand the weight of a man. From the blacksmith, they ordered iron pegs, nails, bars, and a pulley. And from the carpenter they bought a whole stack of wooden planks.

The workers of Langlade who had been contracted to help build Apipolis were very doubtful that such a project could be finished before the Autumn. But Loiseul handed out several thousand francs and kept saying:

'With a little bit of money and a lot of determination nothing is impossible!'

The work went on all Summer. They had ten men working round the clock, digging out the rock with picks, erecting scaffolding, driving iron bars into the rockface and putting the wicker hives into their chalky cells. But of bees, there was no trace.

Each time Léopold went to see them, he would observe all this activity in a distant but amused sort of way. But sooner or later he couldn't help pointing to the engineer who'd be busy directing proceedings:

'That man is going to be the ruin of you!'

Which wasn't too far from the truth.

But wasn't quite right either.

By September, the construction of Apipolis was finished. The news that the engineer and the beekeeper had finally achieved their goal spread like wild fire around Langlade. As did the news that they had run up such debts in the process that the repayments would go on well into the next century. That wasn't true at all. Well not exactly.

In fact, the initial sum of ten thousand gold francs hadn't even covered a quarter of the final cost. So in order to finish the work, they had been forced to borrow a large sum from the bank in Arles, promising the creditors a share in the profits of Apipolis.

'These people are sharks,' grumbled Hippolyte before reluctantly accepting their conditions.

'It is a bit of a risk,' agreed Aurélien. 'But I have a good feeling about all this.'

And so the two men had signed.

Now, on this September morning, the risk had been somewhat reduced. The beekeeper, who had himself played a considerable part in the engineer's crazy scheme, shouted:

'You did it!'

'Not me,' replied Hippolyte. 'It was your idea.'

The two men grinned at each other and shook hands.

'Tomorrow I'll go to Arles and pick up the bees,' said Hippolyte as he stood looking at Apipolis. 'I've ordered them from all the beekeepers in the region. Over a hundred colonies, which will soon fill all the hives of Apipolis. You wait! By next Spring, we'll have thousands and thousands of bees. It will be an amazing sight.'

'How much will all this cost?' asked Aurélien.

'A fortune. But money is irrelevant. We need the best bees we can get.'

'So how much money will we have left after that?'

Hyppolyte took the ever-dwindling wad of notes from his pocket, put most of it to one side and said:

'Enough for a drink at Clovis'!'

Hippolyte Loiseul was true to his word. When he returned from Arles he brought with him enough bees to fill all the hives of Apipolis. It was a spectacle that no one in Langlade would ever forget. Holding the reins of a cart laden with wicker beehives, he made his entrance in the village obscured by a cloud of bees, a buzzing, swirling cloud in the midst of which it was only just possible for the crowd to make out the shape of the engineer.

'It is an apparition!' cried one of the villagers.

Aurélien was the first to welcome Loiseul. Hearing these words made him think of another apparition he had seen once, in Africa. He climbed up onto the cart and the two men took the road to the farmhouse, followed by a troop of children and bees that the presence of so many excitable humans around them had made particularly lively.

Aurélien and Hippolyte placed each beehive carefully into one of the cells, and then, as night fell, and each bee had rejoined its colony, they sat on the rim of the well and looked up at Apipolis. Loiseul lit one of his cigars and said contentedly:

'Now, we just have to wait for all this to be transformed into gold! Winter will be long. But no matter. You will have it in the end, your land of the bees! Bigger and more beautiful than anything you could have seen in Africa. And heaps, what am I saying, mountains of honey will drip on our heads!'

'Yes,' said Aurélien watching the sun disappearing beneath the horizon, 'it is always at springtime that there are new beginnings.'

The Winter passed slowly. It snowed very little. Each morning the two men went to the bottom of the cliff and stared up at it in silence. The bees were deep inside, sleeping in the warmth of Apipolis.

'We mustn't disturb them,' Hippolyte would say.

Then the two of them would go back down to the village and play cards with Clovis.

But Léopold never went with them. He thought the pair of them were mad. Especially the engineer. It was almost as if he knew deep down that he really was mad and yet, for some reason he seemed to be proud of it.

When Spring arrived, it was time to go back to work. And the dream began one April morning, when the first bee took off in search of a flower.

The beekeeper and the engineer had got up well before dawn and were standing at the bottom of the cliff like a couple of excitable children. As they were watching, a single bee emerged from its hive and flew off into the sky. The two of them looked at each other and burst out laughing.

'Luck!' shouted Hippolyte in his booming voice. 'Luck is smiling on us!'

Within a few minutes, the sky was dark with bees. There were millions of them flying around.

'Come on,' said Hippolyte. 'Let's go and have a drink with Clovis. The bees are working for us now.'

Léopold still didn't approve of the whole thing, and the engineer's antics didn't really help. One day, Hippolyte Loiseul took a queen bee and put it on his chin. Within a few moments, thousands of drones had come to join it, settling on his chin and giving the engineer a magnificent beard of bees. He went strutting around Langlade with his wondrous beard, alive and buzzing.

'Strange man,' murmured Léopold.

'That's why I like him,' said Aurélien.

All that Spring, the bees gathered nectar from the flowers of Langlade. And as they did so, they produced a strange and wonderful music.

Aurélien Rochefer loved their endless harmony, even if it was a little lacking in variation. But to him it was far from monotonous. It had its own silences, and sighs, and he found it utterly entrancing.

He loved their music so much that he had ended up giving it a name. He called it: 'The Opera of the Bees'.

At last, the day of the first harvest arrived.

It was a day of celebration to which the whole village was invited. Loiseul wanted everyone to be there to witness this great display of his genius. Léopold and Clovis were the guests of honour, seated like a couple of old senators in the front seats. Behind them in a dense crowd, all the inhabitants of Langlade were staring up in amazement.

A petrified Aurélien was suspended in a basket from the top of the cliff, awaiting the engineer's instructions. And Pauline, who had graciously agreed to take part in this madness, was waiting at the bottom, beside an enormous furnace.

The engineer cleared his throat and began his speech:

'Ladies and gentlemen of Langlade, I welcome you all here today to take part in a most remarkable performance. I beg your utmost attention. For the spectacle in which you will have the honour of assisting in a few minute's time is an opera which requires absolute silence. There will be only one performance, and this is it. The performance you are about to witness is a worldwide premiere. So now, for your delectation and enjoyment it is my great pleasure to present: 'The Opera of Honey, and Silence!"

The engineer raised his hand, and waited a few moments for the whispers and chattering to die down. Then, when the anticipation was almost unbearable, with a sudden graceful gesture like a conductor instructing the orchestra to play the first note, he lowered his hand. And with that, the most silent opera in the world began.

First came the woodwind section. At the bottom of the cliff, Pauline opened the door of the furnace in which some jute sacks had been set alight. The smoke produced travelled upward along an intricate network of pipes that resembled an organ, to the openings of the beehives. And just as the engineer had requested, all this took place in absolute silence. A white, silent opera.

Then the strings began to take up the melody. Aurélien, suspended in the basket in his beekeeper's overalls, pulled on a rope and began lowering himself down the front of the rockface. When he reached the level of the first beehive, he removed the lid, took out a square of wax filled with honey and squeezed it between his hands.

Then it was the time for the brass section to play their part. The honey dripped into a metal vessel and then, like a tiny golden river, it passed through a system of rollers, and was filtered through a mesh, before finally flowing all the way down to the bottom of the cliff.

And all of this took place in utter silence.

Until the final note. The golden note. When the first drop of honey dripped into a glass jar.

The engineer, like a true conductor, lowered his arm, and stood perfectly still. An explosion of joy erupted from the crowd. All the inhabitants of Langlade were laughing with happiness.

'A miracle!' shouted Clovis. 'Bravo, Mr Engineer!'

'The man's from another planet!' thundered Léopold.

'It was a beautiful opera,' said Aurélien throwing himself into his friend's arms.

The engineer looked at him with an infinite tenderness in his eyes.

'Yes, it was perfect. It's been a long time since I've heard such beautiful music!'

The rumour that two men had made a fortune from honey was soon known throughout Provence.

'Who are they?' people would ask.

'A beekeeper and an engineer. You know, the two that came back from Africa.'

'Ah,' would come the reply, 'you mean the dreamer and the eccentric!'

89

It took just two months for Hippolyte Loiseul to go from being considered an eccentric to being considered simply a fool. And for Aurélien Rochefer from being considered a dreamer, to being considered a scatter-brain.

Two months. The time it takes for a lavender flower to open, to blossom in the sun, and then to fade, without any nectar ever being gathered from it.

Two months. The time to see the wonder of Apipolis reduced to a desolate ruin, a disaster that could only have begun in the wayward minds of its two creators.

Two months. The time for the wax moth a tiny, voracious parasite, to destroy all their hard work.

The *Galleria Mellonella*, commonly known as the wax moth, is a parasite that feeds on wax.

The female lays tiny yellow eggs which turn into caterpillars just eight days later, and three weeks after that into chrysalises. After fifteen days the chrysalis becomes a moth. And so the cycle goes on.

The wax moth attacks not only the honeycombs, but the frames and the whole structure of the beehive as well.

When Aurélien and Hipolyte went to check on the beehives shortly before the second harvest, they discovered that in three of the hives instead of the bees all that was left was a heap of dead larvae.

'The wax moth!' cried Aurélien.

'Don't worry. I'd already thought about that.'

The engineer tried to isolate the affected beehives from those that were still healthy. But the insidious disease had already taken hold, and it spread at incredible speed.

A week later, the number of infected beehives had grown to seven. Eight days later, there were more than twenty. After two months, not a single beehive in the whole of Apipolis had escaped the disease.

Hippolyte Loiseul had foreseen everything in his great treatise on beekeeping. Everything apart from fate. And fate didn't want him to become a genius.

When the two men realised that they had lost everything, they tried to gather what little honey they could still save from the disaster.

After filtering it, only a hundred kilos were left. A hundred glass jars, all labelled:

Lavender honey
Apipolis
Langlade
Aurélien Rochefer, beekeeper

Aurélien sold ninety pots, gave seven away, gave two to Hippolyte, and kept just one for himself, which he never opened.

When the news spread, the creditors were drawn like flies to a honeypot. They demanded so much money that Hippolyte's head was in such a spin that he even forgot to puff on his ever-present cigar.

'So how much do we owe these parasites, then?' asked Loiseul.

Aurélien did some calculations, scribbled a figure on a piece of paper and showed it to him.

'As much as that?'

The beekeeper nodded.

'In that case, there is nothing we can do. Except hope for gold to rain down from the sky.'

Hippolyte Loiseul sat down next to a beehive and, in complete despair, he waited for some angel to come and save him from this disaster.

'I don't know about the sky,' said Aurélien. 'But Africa…'

And he went to fetch one of the golden bees he still had left.

Once it was sold, the two men were able to pay off most of Apipolis' debts and get rid of the creditors. Then, with the money that was left, all seventy-seven francs of it, they went down to Clovis' and got drunk for the rest of the night.

III

Hippolyte Loiseul left Langlade one September morning in 1894. He no longer smoked cigars, but he still wore an elegant straw hat. His heart was full of sorrow and his eyes that once brimmed with laughter, were now touched with sadness.

'I'm going to write another book,' he said. 'Only this time, I won't forget the wax moth. In fact, I'm going to compile an exhaustive list of all the illnesses that can affect bees and find cures for them all.'

'Even if you never get round to writing this book,' said Aurélien, 'Apipolis was a still beautiful idea.'

'It was beautiful, wasn't it?' said Hippolyte, nodding. 'Even if you can never have the same dream twice, I will remember ours. Forever.'

For once, Loiseul was lost for words. He squeezed Aurélien's hand, then he turned and went away.

Leopold Rochefer died in the Spring of 1895.

Aurélien had a blue marble gravestone made for him. In his coffin he placed a sprig of lavender. He missed his grandfather very much. He thought of him every day, but he never visited the cemetery in Langlade. For him, Leopold was less present in that rectangle of grey crosses than he was in the blue flowers in the fields.

1895 was a bad year for the lavender harvest. There was a terrible drought, and in the fields the flowers faded one by one.

Aurélien decided to give up cultivating lavender and sold off part of the farm. He spent more and more time indoors thinking about Africa.

One night he dreamt about the young woman with the golden skin, about Makonnen, and about his travelling companions. When he woke up he had the realisation that nothing and no one could ever be forgotten. Least of all those we have loved.

Especially his grandfather. And Hippolyte Loiseul, the craziest and wisest among them.

'What about Apipolis? What are you going to do

with it?' asked Clovis one day. 'The hives have been rotting away in the sun and rain for almost a year now.'

Aurélien looked at what was left of the engineer's project and said sadly:

'I'm going to leave them there and watch them fade away.'

But, even as he said these words he knew that the beauty of their dream would never fade.

One Winter's day while the snow was falling silently, Pauline found a strange parcel in front of her door. There was no note with it, nor any sign of where it had come from. In fact there weren't even have any stamps on it.

Intrigued, she took it inside and closed the door. After a while she unwrapped it. Inside was a beautiful painting. The portrait of a woman with skin the colour of gold.

For the rest of that day she kept thinking about Aurélien and began to miss him terribly. That night she hardly slept at all.

In the morning she sat down to write him a letter. But the words wouldn't come. So without even pausing to snatch up her coat, she went out into the snow and ran all the way to the Rochefers' farm.

Aurélien was about to finish his seventh beehive when Pauline pushed open the door to his workshop. Despite all the setbacks, he had decided to start beekeeping again. Although on a smaller scale this time. He didn't know if he would succeed, if he could protect himself from the ravages of fire, or the wax moth, or anything else that fate could throw at him.

On this occasion he decided to make the beehives out of wood. It was the first time it had been done. They didn't look like hives he'd seen anywhere else. For the beekeeper was no longer an impossible dreamer, but he had lost none of his originality.

While he was painting the seventh beehive a deep golden-yellow colour, Pauline came into the workshop.

She watched him working, then went over to him and said:

'All those years you were in Africa you never wrote me a single letter. And since you've been back, you've scarcely said a word to me. All you cared about was your bees. And now, you send me a portrait. Without so much as a note.'

'Maybe it's too late to write to you now, or to try and tell you...'

She drew closer to him and tilted his head to look into her eyes.

'It is never too late for anything,' she said.

Aurélien took her hand and held it in his.

Pauline eventually freed herself from his grip, and walked towards a shelf at the other end of the room. There were five things on that shelf.

'They are all I have left,' said Aurélien. 'A pot of honey, a golden bee, a notebook of poems, a book about Africa, and a single sprig of lavender.'

She turned back, she flashed him a smile, and answered:

'You're lucky. I have nothing left of you at all. Apart from the portrait you have just given me.'

Pauline stroked the sprig of lavender, glanced scornfully at the jewel, read a poem at random, and picked up the pot of honey. She opened it, dipped her finger in the sweet liquid and brought it to her lips.

'Gathering this honey is possibly the best thing you have done with your life.'

She dipped her finger into the pot, and tasted the honey again.

'The gold of life,' she said.

Aurélien laid down his paintbrush on the workbench. Then he picked up the book about Africa and handed it to her.

'Take it, this book is for you. And all the rest as well. The honey, the golden bee, the notebook of poems, the sprig of lavender. Everything that is left of me, everything I was unable to give you before.'

'For me? Are you sure?'

He looked up at her and saw something he had never seen before. The one thing that had always deeply troubled him. Pauline was gazing in wonder at a drop of honey that was dripping slowly down the side of the jar. And the colour of the honey was reflected in her eyes, her skin, and her outstretched hand.

Aurélien understood that he was standing in front of the woman he had been looking for all his life.

'Now I am certain of it,' he said.

And he felt a deep contentment because he had finally found the gold he had been seeking.

the End

also by Maxence Fermine:

snow

'Yuko Akita had two passions.
Haiku.
And snow.'

£5.99 ISBN 0-953405-3-1

---

the black violin

Napoleon's Army enters Venice. Among them is
Johannes Karelsky whose ambition is to compose the
most beautiful opera ever written.

£6.99 ISBN 0-953405-6-6

All titles are available direct from

acorn book company
PO Box 191, Tadworth
Surrey KT20 5YQ

POST FREE IN THE UK

Cheques payable to acorn book company.
or email your order to sales@acornbook.co.uk

acorn book company

is an independent
publisher of small, high quality editions.

We also operate a mail order web-site.

For more information
please visit us at:
www.acornbook.co.uk